Sanctuary

Sanctuary

A Tale *of*
Life *in the* Woods

Paul Monette

Illustrations by Vivienne Flesher

alyson books
los angeles | new york

MANUFACTURED IN THE UNITED STATES OF AMERICA
DESIGNED BY DEBORAH KERNER

THIS PAPERBACK EDITION IS PUBLISHED BY ALYSON PUBLICATIONS,
P.O. BOX 4371, LOS ANGELES, CALIFORNIA 90078-4371.

FIRST EDITION PUBLISHED IN HARDCOVER BY SCRIBNER: 1997
FIRST PAPERBACK EDITION PUBLISHED BY ALYSON BOOKS: NOVEMBER 1999

99 00 01 02 03 **a** 10 9 8 7 6 5 4 3 2 1

ISBN 1-55583-531-7
(PREVIOUSLY PUBLISHED WITH ISBN 0-684-83286-0 BY SCRIBNER.)

LIBRARY OF CONGRESS CATALOGING-IN-PUBLICATION DATA
MONETTE, PAUL.
SANCTUARY: A TALE OF LIFE IN THE WOODS/BY PAUL MONETTE.
I. TITLE.
PS3563.O523S26 1997
813'.54—DC20   96–30551 CIP

Special thanks to
Star Black, Jenny Dossin, John Fontana,
Leigh Haber, Dan Luckenbill, Robert Monette,
Kristina Nwazota, David Schorr,
Wendy Weil, and Winston Wilde.

Editor's Note

"THE WITCHES AND SHAMANS AND MAGI OF OUR
common heritage seem to cry out for the flesh of nar-
rative," wrote Paul Monette in his original proposal
for the tale that would become *Sanctuary*. The story
would be a departure for this writer, whose work had
always been firmly grounded in the real and present
day. Yet whether they are two female animals brave
enough to love each other, or a witch who longs simply to sustain her forest's safety and secure her own
happiness, the creatures of *Sanctuary* manifest the
themes and preoccupations that infuse all of Paul
Monette's work: the quest for justice; the fluidity of
sexual identity; and the ability of forthright romance
to remake the world. Renarda the Fox and Lapine the
Rabbit, the Witch and Albertus the goofy young

wizard—all are intimately related to the character of their creator, who spent most of his adult life living on the steep side of a canyon in Los Angeles, writing novels, poetry, and prose that helped redefine contemporary ideas of gay love, romantic honesty, and courage in the face of AIDS—the disease that claimed Paul Monette on February 10, 1995. He was forty-nine.

Sanctuary was intended to be part of a collection of tales and essays which, in blurring the boundaries of memoir and magic, might have fused the luminosity of Paul Monette's autobiographical writing with the imaginings of his poetry and fiction. He meant the style of this fable to be "something closer to the dreams, tales, and the myth fragments of Borges, or the exquisite animal stories of Randall Jarrell, especially *Bat-Poet*." *Sanctuary* combines the brilliant, offhand precision of Paul Monette's prose and the demands of the forms of fantasy—along with the passion of his politics. "It's been on my mind for a long time," he wrote, "that there aren't enough tales and fables that take into account the gay and lesbian experience, both the tragic and the exalted. Ours is a mythology invisible to history. Thus I would love to fashion a story or two worthy of being told around the tribal campfire."

Sanctuary has been minimally edited for clarity and resonance. The spirited ghostliness of Vivienne Flesher's illustrations provides the story with additional vividness and vision.

Perhaps what is most enchanting about this story is the very possibility of enchantment itself. Protecting the primeval forest from everything except the justices of nature, and creating a space safe for all kinds of love, the Spell in *Sanctuary* works "by changing minds." Which was the way the Spell's true creator, Paul Monette, worked as well.

DAVID GROFF

Sanctuary

IT MAY NOT HAVE BEEN—how could it have been?—the very last forest. But to all the creatures who lived there—both the descendants of the First Ones, down and down the path of the seasons, and the later ones who came there to settle, seeking refuge—it *felt* as though all the other forests had disappeared, right down to the last leaf, and they were precious and alone.

Not that the animals spent much time thinking about it, thinking being the very thing the forest freed them from. What they had instead, and it was all they really needed, was the instinct of ancestry, of knowing who they were, whether they'd come to be here before the Spell or after. The generations of the young couldn't have even told you what the Spell was, but all the same they knew in their bones where they fit in the order of things: before or after.

When the Spell rang down on the forest, it didn't come with a clang like a gong, or the shut of an iron gate. It fell like rain on a cloudless day, a fine cool mist, and then it was one with the morning dew. And so it was done without any single living thing knowing what had happened. Not a blade of grass stopped swaying in the open fields. Nothing altered even slightly its natural pattern—not the honeybee's nose-dive as it fell upon a sunflower, not the fox's final scramble overtaking the hare. Most of life slept through it, dozing like a grove of pitch pine. If the witch was at all proud of how she'd created the Spell, it was the stealth of the thing that satisfied her most.

The witch had lived in the forest since before the world told time. It was all hers. Or his—for some mornings the witch was a man, some mornings a woman. Yet she wasn't possessive, not even a bit. In her ageless heart she was glad to share the least inch of her vast domain with the tiniest of the white-spotted

birds and the teeming anthills; with bear and ferret, puma, the dueling elk, the spider's loom, moss on every side of every trunk—all of them free. She and the forest set forth no rules but life itself.

Still, she kept her distance. Not for her the pursuit of a scattering of seed on a log, or bubbles rising from a dripping spring, or drying fruit among the roots of the burrow where she resided. A solitary spirit, she didn't seek connection with her creatures, and that was that. None of the forest animals took offense, bound as they were on errands all their own. They didn't care that she never named them or hadn't a clue which was female, which was male. She didn't notice the babies in the spring, or the old ones going off to die in a glade of bones. It was all the same to her: the world outside. Uncategorized, uncensused. Everything let be.

But *inside*—within the star-shot dome of her magic, where the weather was always changing, night and day a silver blur, the wheel of years spinning at the speed of light, there in the center of all the seeming and the phantasms—she beheld the phenomenal world with the ice-cold moon of second sight. Nothing anywhere escaped her watchfulness. Not the felling of trees in a thousand forests near and far from hers, not the crack of a hunter's single shot straying close to her invisible borders.

As the waterfall of decades spilled and spilled, unstoppable, she knew how the other forests were thinning. Slashed and burned. Hauled away, square miles at a stretch, to be rendered into toothpicks. The cleared land was farmed and squandered till the soil died of its own exhaustion. Desert lay where everything green had grown.

To protect her own realm required spells of greater and greater intensity. It wasn't enough anymore to fix it so the hunter fell on his shotgun, blowing a hole in his clumsy heart. Or to pin the farmer's eldest son beneath a crashing oak, breaking him in half so that his clearing days were over. It couldn't be just a single spell anymore, one on one, the barest blink of a witch's eye, like swatting away a pesky gnat.

No, now it required the whole of her. She would sit all day outside the hollow tree trunk of her burrow, her eyes transfixed at some spot of light that only she could see, as her bottomless mind conjured and assembled. With a white-hot force of will, burning like phosphorus, she could feel an invisible shield wrap itself tighter around the outer limits of her woodlands. Stronger than barbed wire shot through with a lethal current, yet in thickness hardly the breadth of an atom.

But most of the time the spell did not work by maiming, or in physically repelling interlopers— It worked by changing minds. Whenever intruders moved to enter the forest—hunter, hermit, sasquatch, explorer, migrant herd, seeker of ore—their heads would fill with an inkling of fear, a looming beast just out of sight in the trees. Their most appalling secret terror taking physical form, come to corner them at last. And then they would have a sudden change of heart. They'd turn and follow a different trail, the spoor of a different prey, aiming elsewhere their guns, their dousing rods, and their Geiger counters.

It gave her huge satisfaction to watch them all go away. But it grew harder every day, it seemed, to summon up this barrier spell, a fearful concentration of her powers. Soon she had no time left for anything else. And when it came to that, the overwork and the overtime, she lost her precious repose. No longer could she allow room for the desultory tricks of a Tuesday morning in June, magic running through her fingers like a sweet cascade of coins.

Now she found herself prey to the old sad thoughts the forest had long since managed to clear from her head—namely, how could she be the only witch she knew? Where were the others? It stood to reason they were everywhere about—among other forests, other weathers—as populous as any other creature of the woods. But if they were out there, they never made any attempt to connect, even by way of their magic. Part of the reason she woke some days as a man was just to lend a little variety to her acquaintance.

And anyway, the man was just herself in another form, not really other at all. In truth, she was more or less a man/woman without even trying. Sometimes she enjoyed her body as if it held a pair of souls, warring and now uniting, or as if one side were dreaming the other.

Yet here was the cruel jest of the very flux she embodied: she could never fall in love with herself. For she required not another version of her body but the Other, the Other who never came. The more she thought about it, the sadder she got. Especially now, with the Spell of the forest shield tearing at her, clawing for more of her essence. She who never so much as noticed the coupling of the animals suddenly noticed almost nothing else.

Even the Great Horned Owl who perched in the

top of the tree above her head, the owl who had been her familiar since the beginning, wasn't any real comfort or very good company. He mostly kept to his perch except when he hunted at night. He was reasonably good as a sentry, though not so good as the witch's own second sight, and thus not even necessary to her. Besides, he was taciturn and distinctly uncommunicative. His never-ending double "Who"— the hollowness of the tone, its vast disinterest— sometimes nearly drove her mad. It always seemed he was taunting her in her solitude, as if the sole response to the din of "Who . . . Who?" was the Other she couldn't reach.

The palest blue of summer twilight settled on the forest. The creature sounds of the day went hushed, as if everything alive was holding its breath. She could not reach out and feel her forest as she used to, because the Spell that held its borders throbbed in her temples like migraine. She understood at last where all of this was headed. And the tears came, silent, unconsolable. It was either herself or the Spell that could thrive, it could not be both. She had to give over the very core and wellspring of her powers, until she was left as dry and empty as a milkweed pod at the brink of winter.

She'd always assumed she couldn't die, though no one had ever told her as much. But hers was not to be an immortality of the body, after all. Her claim on lasting forever resided in the Spell alone. Yet she never complained or balked as this knowledge dawned on her. In the last weeks she lay down on the bed of the forest floor, letting fallen leaves and husks and faded blossoms blow over her into a blanket. In this way she conserved the laser of the Spell, letting it seep from the cracks of her heart, stronger and stronger as she lay spent, a husk herself and sometimes near delirious.

As a grudging sort of honor guard, the horned owl swooped from the treetop to the ground, standing sentry at the witch's head. He didn't much like to see her shiver and convulse, or listen to the incoherent raving of her incantations. But it was his job to be there, and he didn't shirk it. If he worried what would happen to the enchantment of the place once she was gone, he tried not to think that far ahead. Yet he took a certain secret pleasure in assuming *he* would take on the forest's soul in her stead. "Who . . . Who?" he asked as he watched her energy drain from her. The heir to all her power, that's who.

It was just about then—as she faded, growing

indistinguishable from the leafmeal where she lay—
that random gaps began to appear in the border
shield. It would happen when she was dreaming of
the Other, averting momentarily the intense gaze of
the moon inside her. And through those gaps rushed
animals by the thousands, suddenly sensing a win-
dow of escape from the dwindling trees of their own
dying habitats, like a spring migration into the up-
lands, where the grass grew fresh and the streams
were full. Of course they didn't understand they were
entering a magic refuge, nor did they have the slightest notion of the Spell they burrowed under like a
fence. Wave upon wave of deer leapt through the
rents in the seamless curtain. A hundred flights of
birds shadowed the trees below as they crowded
through the chinks in the air.

Even in her fevered dreaming, bidding good-
bye to love, the witch had a *second* second sight of the
new arrivals, and accepted them and blessed them. At
her most disconnected, howling at her own moon
like a she-wolf, she never permitted a hunter through
the gaps, never a greedy woodsman, never a prospec-
tor for gold.

Soon there was next to nothing left of her, just
another pile of last year's leaves, but the sacrifice of

her essence had left the border shield gleaming like a wall of diamond, invisible and impenetrable forever. The owl rose up with a flap of his enormous wings, regaining his perch at the tree's summit. He had a lot to mull over, and all the time in the world to do it.

OTHERWISE, the denizens of the forest barely noticed the change. They'd never been especially conscious of the witch when she was alive, and certainly felt no gratitude for the magic that had protected them. They knew no other reality but the one she'd engineered for them. It may have been that the oldest of the First Ones still remembered what a hunter was, or a lumberjack—some primal shiver of fear they couldn't shake. But now that the threat had long since dissipated, the shiver instinct had atrophied, seeping away like the shrillest warning notes of birdsong.

As the years cascaded by as swift as ever, the birds and animals moved through a world where there was nothing external to fear, taking it all for granted. As for the refugees of the witch's final days— knowing exactly the sort of cruelty and haplessness they'd managed to escape—they counted themselves absurdly lucky. They quickly banished all thought of the past, and passed nothing on to their children's children. Thus they thought they could fit in unnoticed, as rooted in the forest as the trees themselves.

And anyway, the creatures of the forest weren't immortal either. They might not have to fear the arrow and the bullet, but otherwise they went down in their own time. The predators preyed as always. Bears mauled bees' nests to scoop out a fistful of honey. Wolves overtook and devoured deer. Hawks dropped on field mice. Badgers smashed birds' eggs, sucking the yolk off their paws. Snakes swallowed hedgehogs whole. Danger lay round the next bend, always. Even if the witch could have granted them something like life eternal, she wouldn't have dreamed of doing so. She had always known their lives together were run by rounds and cycles, that if nothing died then nothing would ever be renewed.

Still, the animals could hardly be faulted for being ignorant of the overriding enchantment of the Spell. They experienced it rather in glints and flashes—a momentary lull in the frenzy of the hunt, a quiet drink in a woodland pool, lazing the afternoon away sprawled in the sun on a boulder. Sometimes life seemed enchanted all on its own—no source required, no origin. They didn't need a reason any more than they needed to know they would die, or why they never migrated in the winter.

So it seemed particularly unnecessary when the call went out announcing a general gathering, to be held the night of the next full moon. It passed like a whisper to every den and nest, to every hunting ground. Most of the inhabitants of this last forest didn't even know what a gathering was. They'd never gathered before. Even the witch had never felt the need to bring them all together. A bad idea, as she would've been the first to say.

Therefore, it wasn't surprising that the whole forest sniffed with contempt at the very notion of congregating, species by species. They knew the rigid hierarchy of their orders in the forest. Where a creature stood in the scheme of things was implicit in being a grizzly, a chipmunk, a crow. Were they really expected to stand shoulder to shoulder with those who were weaker than they? Besides, there wasn't the merest mite or lichen that didn't feel superior to *something* else, even if its comparative worth was all a delusion. To bring them together seemed unnatural, like molting in the wrong season. Of all the things they didn't need, it was self-examination—worse, self-knowledge.

But once they heard the source of the call, that it had issued direct from the Great Horned Owl, they had instant second thoughts. For the owl at the crest of the tallest spruce had grown to be a sort of unacknowledged spirit of the place. No one could have said why, nor did anyone acknowledge this role as anything but ceremonial. In all the river of years that had passed since the witch's decline, the horned owl never so much as blinked. He didn't appear to require any homage. In truth, he didn't appear to notice anybody else, save for the mice he swooped down on for his nightly feeding. He might have been a statue otherwise.

Yet behind his wide unblinking face, the owl was busy: he was mulling. Unceasingly, ever since the witch's final sigh among the leaves, ceding her strength to the forest shield, he had been pondering the forest and his role in it. For the longest time, the owl had been content to wait for the passing of the magic from the witch's hands to his own dark and feathered self. He had been readying himself for sorcery and the fire of change, the power that would drip from his claws like the blood of his mousy prey. It had taken him forever to recognize that as the witch's longtime familiar he wasn't ever going to possess the witch's force. For the owl there would be no special dispensations, no sudden transformations, especially no second sight.

He disdained this fact. Rejected it. Cursed it. Seethed with rage. But none of his fury brought him any closer to the place of power he thought he deserved. Not that he didn't have a superior sense of *first* sight, eyes so sharp he could see across the treetops to the very borders of the forest. He would perch atop the spruce utterly motionless, except for the slow swivel of his horned head, turning full circles like a lighthouse. He thus kept watch over the whole domain of the forest he lacked the magic to control.

He still would've observed any attempted trespass of the outer limits. Any stray hunter, any lumberjack crew. But the Spell had worked so exceedingly well for so long that no one even bothered to venture near the forest anymore. The last forest had finally been forgotten by the world beyond, in its ceaseless round of tearing down and churning up, till the wasteland they made was all they knew.

With the Spell so locked in place, the owl in all his grandeur merely served as sentry. Ceremonial indeed, since he had no power, but to him at least a full-time job. And he was galled by a mounting sense of dread he couldn't name. It came from the south-west quarter beyond the forest, a place of dusty, scrub-covered hills where no drop of water ever fell. The owl could see for himself that there was no break in the shield, and yet a hot and prickly wind had commenced to blow from that direction.

Probably he was the only one to sense it, perched as he was at the highest summit of the trees. But he could feel it intensely, a wind that riffled and scorched the feathers of his left wing. Dried his left eye till it flecked with red and teared and blinked, cutting his vision in half.

Soon he was filled with a terrible panic. For here was the scalding evidence of his powerlessness, proof he possessed no special spirit. The witch would've known without batting an eye the source of the desert wind. Her second sight would've soared beyond the forest borders and across the barren wastes. If the wind had portended danger, she would've known in an instant whether it was hunters or a plague of locusts, an angry god or an evil sorcerer. The poor horned owl, with the hot wind tickling his ear, could only blindly speculate.

But he'd mulled long enough—generations now—that he knew it was time to act. He would act even if his power was only *seeming*—or what the world beyond the forest called *political*. So he spread his great fanning wings and swooped to the forest floor below. In a short few minutes a beaver and a raccoon came tearing through the trees on either side to do his bidding. For they were *his* familiars. There existed not a smidgen of power between them, but all the same they exhibited a puffing sort of pride, just to bear the rank of the owl's lieutenants.

"Go and tell all the animals," the owl hooted imperiously, "from everything that flies to all that worm under the ground. Announce that we will all gather together on the plain of the river valley at the stroke of the next full moon. Make sure you tell them *who*"—the word tolled like a dark bell, and he could not help but repeat it—"*who* has called the gathering."

The beaver and the raccoon nodded in dumb unison. They were both too timid, or else too proud, to say they hadn't a clue what gathering meant. But they turned on their heels abruptly and fanned out east and west, spreading the word. The wheeling birds cavorting in the autumn sky above picked up the gist and bore it north and south, till all the forest was blanketed with the owl's inscrutable order.

Oh, they continued to grumble and grouse, the

higher species especially. They didn't want to leave their dens and killing grounds. They resisted mightily the very notion of mingling herds on the plain, even for just one night. They didn't see how they would stop the bloody clashes, the collision of teeth, paws, a thousand antlers. What was going to prevent them all from trying to stake new territory, or even worse, from plunging into the ranks of their helpless prey? Why wouldn't the cougars massacre the deer, brought together like some delirious feast of plenty? How would that horned owl keep order when every creature's instinct was to maul and feed on the creature just below?

The mass of them decided to attend the gathering for that very reason, almost daring the owl to make it work. If it didn't, why then they would have a field day of carnage—and perhaps establish in the process who in fact were the kings of the forest, the unconquerables. From the outer reaches of the woodlands, the herds and packs began the long trek when the harvest moon was hardly a quarter risen, a beckoning curl of orange. They tramped through the tight-knit trees and across the wildflower glades, forded the brooks, and foraged in the underbrush. They were like numberless ranks of so many armies, all their powers held in uneasy reserve.

They gathered on the river plain with a remarkable lack of incident, given the potential for explosion. They held their ranks and kept to a tight formation, occupying no more space than was absolutely necessary. If the possums happened to find themselves cheek by jowl with timber wolves or black bears, they all managed a sort of disdain that kept one another at a safe remove.

But more than simple pride was at work, more than a healthy dose of wariness. As they settled into their places with a minimum of snarling and snapping, as they focused their collective gaze at the top of the giant spruce, the disk of the full blood moon seeming to perch at the crest of the plain like a pagan star—they were suddenly interfused with a rapturous glow of serenity, tingling from tip to tail, from the pads of their paws to their quivering ears.

This was the feeling of absolute safety, that utter certainty that they would be protected, no matter what fires and floods and evil winds hurled themselves against the forest shield. An aura of calm pervaded them, one that they'd only experienced before in glimmers and fleeting moments, the unacknowledged legacy of the witch's final spell. But now as they fixed on the moon, the Spell took them over at fullest force, summoning within them an incalculable joy.

And so, when the owl circled his perch, alighting in the topmost branch, the denizens of the last forest naturally thought it was *he* who'd produced the euphoria, this night of freedom from all predations. Who else could they thank but him? Thus did the owl achieve his dearest goal short of real magic: the *illusion* of power. He was of course taking credit for all the witch's labors. And why not? There wasn't a soul around to contradict him.

Silence fell over the valley as the owl settled his wings and puffed up the downy feathers of his snow-white chest. His great eyes reflected the pumpkin orange of the harvest moon above him.

"My honored friends," he began, though the vast crowd would have been hard put to return the greeting honestly. "The time has come to tell you all the forest's secrets. I need your help, each in his own way, to keep us safe forever. And especially I need your alertness and counsel to root out the enemy within."

This last remark he left without elaboration, so the animals looked furtively left and right, wondering which of their number he could mean.

"A thousand moons ago—a thousand thousand—

a sorcerer taught me how to construct an invisible shield of protection around the perimeter of our forest home. It took me years of withering concentration to achieve it—my heart pounding, my head so light I thought I'd tumble off my perch. And I did it all for you, so you would never have to worry again about the dangers massed without. No riflemen, no bowmen, no tremors to crack the ground, no chance that a wayward star would ever fall on us.

"I did all this without the slightest expectation of reward or even gratitude. As some of you may know, the great horned species is notable for its selflessness, its lack of foolish pride."

Now was the moment he expected them to raise a cry of thanksgiving, a cheer that would deafen his radar ears but still be worth a month of ringing in his head. Yet they held their silence as if in thrall to his words, or perhaps not wanting to jar the glow of serenity that enfolded them. The owl decided not to take it personally—very big of him—because he knew he had them in the clutch of his talons. Silence was homage enough, and in the end perhaps more useful than a lot of huzzahs and caterwauling. It showed him they would be his secret spies, not one of them so stiff and obvious as a sentry or a soldier.

Penetrating the enemy ranks with nobody any the wiser.

"Surely you must be asking yourselves why, if your savior and protector is so exceedingly modest, he has chosen this time and place to reveal the benevolence of his sorcery. I will tell you why. But you must go back a thousand thousand moons to understand. When I was conjuring the forest shield, trying to keep the sorcerer's incantations in their proper order—for the slightest deviation would have left us in a desert—I did some stumbling of my own. Yes, even I. I couldn't quite bring all the elements together. Part of my vision was still watching out for mouselets in the field. After all, I had to eat.

"And during that time of mere partial success, when the shield was torn and shredded by a failure of my will, a great group of outsiders managed to slip in. Refugees from forests that scarcely sported a single tree anymore. Exiles. Criminals. All manner of antisocial forces. I was too busy with my magic to even take their count.

"By the time the shield was at last in place, the population of our forest had grown by leaps. That's when I made my big mistake, so exhausted was I from my labors. I should have skimmed the forest and taken note of all the strangers. I should have sent a team to tar their fur with pitch or burn an alien brand, something to keep them always separate, always identifiable."

The animals massed in the river valley stirred uneasily. A ripple of fear seemed to brush their pelts and feathers.

"By now there is no way of knowing, so blended in have the aliens come to be. If I were to ask you all to separate now into two groups—First Ones and refugees—none of you would obey me. Many of you don't even know anymore which your forefathers were. No one is to blame for that."

The owl swept his stiff-necked head from one edge of the plain to another. "But now we find ourselves in a most unpleasant and curious situation: we are too many. The hunting grounds and fishing grounds are dwindling. The air above us is crowded with birds, tangling their formations. Slowly, ever so subtly, this overcrowding is taking its toll. Before we know it our freedoms will begin to fall away, and by then it will be too late."

Again the beasts and birds and bugs shivered with a weird uncertainty. *They* had never felt overcrowded or overpopulated. Every quarter of the forest seemed to support exactly the right amount of life. Were they so much part of the problem they couldn't even *see* the problem? Restlessly the dam bears drew their cubs closer together. The fireflies massed in the lower branches of the willows that lined the river, seeking safety in numbers. The possums began to ease themselves toward the edges of the crowd, broods of babies in tow, deciding they'd heard enough. It was time, the animals began to decide, to go back to their burrows and nests, gathering leaves as they went to camouflage the entrance.

In other words, all the shy and defenseless creatures were biding their time to bolt from the gathering—just as soon as the owl had finished speaking. Already—perhaps because they were such nervous types to begin with, fatalistic before all else—they knew what was coming: a winnowing out. In which case, they knew from long experience that they'd be the first to go. The first to be sacrificed to ease the overcrowding, the first to be sent into exile.

"Tonight," continued the owl, knowing exactly when to resume, now that he'd sown the maximum amount of fear he could, "tonight I am only asking for your vigilance. That you all keep an ear cocked for any behavior that doesn't feel quite right. Anything that might expose . . ." He paused as if to search for the perfect word. ". . . a *differentness*, shall we say. Any clue to a foreign ancestry, an upbringing by outsiders. All suspicions should be reported directly to me."

No longer was the anxious stirring in the crowd confined to the harmless and the easily victimized. Great beasts who lived by their teeth and had no fear of *anything* seemed to be holding their breath. The swift-footed crickets in the tall grass went suddenly silent. Where was all this headed? The spell of safety seemed about to vanish, as all the living things in the enchanted forest would wake up at once, and never even know they'd been asleep.

"Now, I don't want any of you to worry," the owl hastened to reassure them. "There is no plan to punish or even banish the creatures thus reported. It is merely a *cautionary* measure. The overcrowding I speak of is nowhere near the saturation point. But we must have a list in place before we reach the danger level. And then it may be necessary to set aside an overcrowded *zone*, and to fill its forest acreage with creatures from the 'different' list. If such a measure seems unfair to the progeny of the late arrivals, then one of *you* should come up with an alternate plan. But whether we like it or not, wherever the stroke of

fate has placed us in the natural order, we must acknowledge that we are composed of two distinct and
separate classes: First Ones and refugees. There are
certain rights and responsibilities that attach to being
original to the life of this spellbound forest.

"As sorcerer of the Spell, it falls to me to make
the laws. Besides, we will all be a lot better off once
we know who's who. From knowledge of our two
races will come the strength to protect the forest
shield. And then we will be safe forever, each with his
own kind."

With this last rhetorical flourish he had clearly
finished his presentation. He didn't ask for questions.
At the top of the spruce he gave a magnificent treble
hoot and stretched his wings out to their fullest span.
It was by way of a formal dismissal. Within moments
the herds and packs and prides and flocks began to
move, homing back to the reaches of their ancestral
grounds. An eerie silence accompanied them as they
left the plain of the river valley. Few even whispered.
It was as if nobody wished to speculate any further on
the meaning of the owl's blood-moon declaration.
Having arrived at the gathering without the need or
wish for self-knowledge, they left the place in the
same spirit.

. . .

A LONG TIME would pass before anyone responded to the owl's command, but he was quite content to wait. He'd planted the seed. The ill wind still blew from the southwest quarter, but he no longer let it frighten him. He had told the world of the last forest what they had not wanted to know, such that he could count on them for a living shield if that fearful wind grew into a gale. They knew now that he was their leader and protector. What he had accomplished at the gathering, splitting them into two races, was far too subtle for most of them to appreciate.

The antagonism would come in its own time. When the mating season arrived, the stud males would clash as usual—bighorn sheep butting horns; the birds fluffing out their iridescent plumage as they pecked away their rivals—the yearly declarations of primacy.

But here and there a spurned and beaten male would see that he had another option besides licking his wounds. He would make his way to the spruce grove of the owl and whisper a suspicion against his conqueror—a vague but telling accusation of a certain *foreignness*, perhaps a tendency to fight dirty that indicated a low upbringing. Effusive with gratitude,

the owl would turn to his growing list clawed in the bark of the tree, and then he would add the name. The owl would thus restore the pride of the beaten creature and send him off readier than ever to whisper again.

Or the wrens would be busily building nests, gathering twigs and bits of string. And one would notice how another had claimed the safest crook on the leafiest branch. Furious and jealous, the unlucky one would erect her *second-best* nest with redoubled frenzy, even as her envy built as well. Eventually, here was the very wren who would fly off to have an audience with the owl, sputtering rank gossip about the *oddness* of her neighbor with the arrogant nest. She didn't sit her eggs properly; she wasn't friendly with the other wrens. When the eggs finally hatched, she fed the babies with strange food, not the usual bugs and worms. There was definitely something *not right* about that wren.

Soon the owl could count on a near daily parade of snitches and tattlers, working out their private grudges by way of innuendo. The reports of differentness began to reach such a din that the owl was forced to declare fixed times to entertain the betrayers. The hour before dawn, the hour after dusk, chosen so every spy could preserve his anonymity by darkness. By now the whole trunk of the owl's spruce was covered with scratches and hieroglyphs, amounting to a veritable census of second-class citizens, the suspected heirs of refugees.

The owl could not have been more thrilled by the way the forest was turning on itself, but he hadn't found quite the right and provable instance of transgression that could prove his power. He needed a rock-solid break of natural law to begin the real inquisition. Too much of what he had scrawled on the bark was merely innuendo. But as always he was patient. The appropriately scandalous incident would wriggle to the surface soon enough. He simply had to be ready to catch it by the tail. And meanwhile, the doubt and paranoia instilled by the spy network would continue to weaken the independent fiber of life in the forest, making all the creatures ready to be commanded utterly.

IN THE NORTHERN QUARTER of the forest, the first dusting of snow had come early. On a cold bracing morning in mid-November, when the crackling air was thick with the animals' smoky breath, the fox who called herself Renarda was stealthily prowling the brow of the hill, close by a stand of Norway fir. It was early, the snowy ground having just shaken the blue of morning twilight, but Renarda did her best hunting in the hour after dawn.

Suddenly she spotted a stirring at the edge of the copse. Perhaps it was just a branch throwing off its shawl of snow, but Renarda crouched and perked her russet ears, completely still as she watched. Sure enough, the snow-laden undergrowth began to rustle, and a fine fat rabbit emerged into the clearing. Dark brown, almost the color of mink. And instantly alert, of course, her own ears twitching with concentration as she surveyed the surrounding field.

The rabbit, called Lapine, had come into the first real winter of her own—last year having still been part of a brood of little ones, fretted over by its mother. Now she was nursing the habits of independence, exhilarated by the wintry dawn.

But she was too slow to turn her head—so the fox had the advantage as it leapt through the powder drift in hot pursuit. Lapine barely had time to register the species of her attacker, as she bounded away from the safety of the copse and set off across the field leaving a wake of frenzied snow. Their strength and cunning were about equal at the start, trailing zigzag through the upland meadows—Renarda now closing in, Lapine putting a burst on and stretching the distance between them. A predator's game of tag.

In one way, of course, they were perfectly matched, by way of their inexperience. Renarda had been taught all the hunter's right moves by her mother, but had still never brought down any prey of her own. It was a virgin season for both. Perhaps that was why they lengthened the course of the hunt, darting over the ice of a woodland pond, scrambling through brambles, leaping the beavers' dams along the stream.

And perhaps they wouldn't have admitted as much—a thought too radical for a hunter's world— but they were enjoying the chase for its own sake. Playing, almost. Lapine casting a glance over her shoulder, almost locking eyes with the enemy, almost getting the ghost of a smile in return.

In a word: *different.*

They darted and gamboled in the icy air. From the safety of his lair at the roots of a birch tree, an old white bunny grimaced in disapproval as fox and rabbit rushed by. The chase would have gone on for hours, perhaps, till night had shut it down, if Lapine hadn't found herself at a dead-end wall of rock. It was

too sheer to climb, too high to jump. Panting with exertion, Lapine turned to face her hunter, her restless eyes scanning the cul de sac for any way out. Renarda was even more winded as she entered the rock hollow, a stitch stinging in her ribs, panting so she couldn't speak.

The two animals watched each other as they fought for breath. It wasn't clear at what moment their fierce breathing evolved into laughter, but there they both were, like a pair of runners giddy at the finish line. Renarda spoke first, her words more breathed out sharply than spoken. "Excellent chase, Lapine! First class!"

Lapine nodded modestly, acknowledging the compliment. "It was my first time. Solo, that is."

"Imagine that! Such instinct you must have—such power in reserve!"

They seemed to have run out of things to say, but still they stared in one another's eyes. They couldn't seem to look away. Lapine was not about to say "What now?"—for fear the only answer was "Now I eat you."

But Renarda at last glanced away shyly and then seemed to have a new idea. "Look at all the crab apples," she said, gesturing round at the snow. Indeed, a crab apple tree high up on the hill was bare-branched, having shed its fruit among the tumbled rocks. Yellow and red and brown, the knobs of apple peeked out of the snow. And because it was such a windless place, it was the perfect spot for a winter's picnic. Renarda gathered a handful and offered Lapine a seat on a bench of stone.

A moment later they were crouched together, busily chewing fruit. Renarda tended to gobble them up whole, having the right sort of razor teeth for the task. Lapine nibbled contentedly, dicing her way through the apple and consuming succulent bits.

"Tell me, Lapine, do you live around here?" Renarda asked.

"Well, yes," came the modest reply. "Over in the copse of birches where you . . ." She groped for the right word.

". . . where I chased you. Of course. And tell me, Lapine, do you have a mate?"

"No, no. My first mating season will be in the spring." Lapine paused to think for a moment. "I . . . don't think I'm cut out for mating."

"Of course you are. It's in your makeup. But perhaps you don't cotton to the notion of a *mate*, those big buck jackrabbit males that prowl and strut the woods."

"Perhaps," conceded Lapine timidly. "And what about *you*?"

"Oh, I almost had a litter last summer. I had a fox admirer who had clearly chosen me and danced attention for days."

"What did you do?"

Renarda shrugged. "Ran away. I wasn't ready. I was starting to feel the need of something different."

"Different how?"

"Somebody who would suit me more exactly. It took me months to realize it didn't have to be a fox at all. I flirted for a while with a bear, but it was too much of a stretch. Every time she rolled over in bed, she practically crushed me."

Lapine was grave. "But didn't anyone protest? After all, it's against the law."

"You mean the owl's law?" Renarda snorted with contempt. "A little dictator, that one. But yes, we had to be secret, and only meet under cover of dark."

"And are you still . . . looking?"

A long pause, in which there was no sound except the ghostly sloughing of snow from the branches. Renarda turned her tawny eyes on the rabbit, looking at her long and deep. Normally Lapine would have been skittish in the face of so much attention, especially from a fox, but just now she found it a comfort, as if she were warming her paws at a woodland fire. She contented herself to wait for an answer.

And when it came, it was spoken with indescribable tenderness. "I don't think I'm looking anymore," Renarda said in a husky whisper. With that she leaned over Lapine and planted a kiss on her lips, stroking the rabbit's shiny fur till Lapine fairly shivered with delight. Then they stretched out and clung to each other mutely, basking in their new and sudden bond.

The love between Lapine and Renarda was not unmixed with the thrill of fear, the consciousness of danger round the next bend in the path, so ubiquitous was the owl's spy network. But for love's sake there really wasn't any choice at all. The risks were part of the challenge, and neither of them was prepared to resist their deepest feelings. Until this moment, Lapine would have said, life in the woods had seemed dreary and meaningless, with no escape but the inevitable crunch of a predator's jaws.

They had to build a lair with a double entrance, for no one must ever see them together in public. Renarda had to become vegetarian, so as not to be seen out hunting, especially by a randy fox. They foraged in separate directions all day long, meeting at dusk in

the lair. And then, how they would groom each other and stroke each other, never tiring of the sighing and the oneness.

They were lucky that the northern quarter was sparsely settled. This part of the forest had no crowds or neighborhoods to speak of, and it was too cold for extended forays into the wilds. Indeed, they might have gotten away with their undiscovered love indefinitely, had it not been for Lapine's romantic presumption about the moon. Late one night, unable to sleep for joy, she popped her head from the burrow and gazed on the moonlit snowscape. It was breathtaking, a plain of shimmering cobalt blue beneath the glitter dome of the winter sky. And the moon itself! Full and bright, achingly pure in the velvet blackness of the night.

She couldn't bear to see so much beauty without Renarda. The fox was a light sleeper anyway, her hind legs more often than not twitching in sleep as she relived the day's runs. She could tell how excited Lapine was as the two of them crawled out into the icy dark. They settled themselves on a hollow log. Leaning there shoulder to shoulder, head to head, they gazed at the moon in silence—unafraid, as if it shone for them alone.

. . .

AS FATE WOULD HAVE IT, the owl himself was on the wing and hunting that moonlit night, his sharp eyes alert for rodents. When he circled above the two figures, Renarda and Lapine in close embrace, he thought at first his eye had tricked him. Surely that fox down there ought to be gnawing the bones of the rabbit, not sitting shoulder to shoulder in blissful contemplation.

Another swoop, lower now, and the owl could see quite clearly that the two were in love. Taking a perch at the top of a birch tree, the owl arranged his wings and stared. He could not of course ascertain at this distance that the two figures were both female. That would have been a whole *other* crime. What he did see was shocking enough: the mingling of two species, an association that challenged all he had decreed to be against the laws of nature as well as the law of magic. It was all the owl could do not to hoot with delight. He'd seen enough. He flew off across the still moonscape, regaining his spot at the top of the spruce, and began to make his delirious plans for the morrow.

Renarda and Lapine didn't even see the danger coming, or realize afterward that doom had suddenly fallen on them. They were both too caught up in the sky's dazzling brightness. They went to bed at last completely unaware of the drama they'd engaged, sleeping in late because they'd been up half the night, and because they couldn't rouse themselves from the cozy warmth of bodily contact. Each of them thought the other's fur the softest thing in the world.

They ate a breakfast of sweet grass, after which Renarda was ready to forage. As usual they would leave the lair five minutes apart, so as to call no attention on them. Renarda kissed Lapine good-bye and headed out into the snow. For the next five minutes, Lapine freshened and fluffed up the bed of leaves where they slept. Then she popped out of the other entrance to the lair, intent on a day of gathering grass and nuts and wild lettuce.

Emerging into the clearing, Lapine knew instantly something was amiss. Renarda was backed against a large oak tree, arguing, hunched and ready to spring, though her stance didn't seem to intimidate her two interlocuters. For the beaver and the raccoon had cornered her the moment she left the lair. The owl's two familiars were there to issue a warrant for Renarda's and Lapine's arrest. Renarda was spitting and snarling at them, but they did not budge.

"What's wrong?" asked a plaintive Lapine.

"Good, here's the other one," declared the raccoon. He approached Lapine, his eyes slitted with menace. "We're here on official business. The two of you are being charged with crimes against nature. The owl expects you to appear tomorrow to answer these charges."

"Appear *where?*" demanded a bewildered Lapine.

"At the owl's spruce grove," snapped Renarda. "We've been called before the owl's kangaroo court."

Lapine was devastated; they had been so careful to avoid harm's way, and now their wintry idyll would be over. But Renarda went on, sneering at the beaver

and the raccoon. "You're just lackeys. How do you in-
tend to get us there? I've a good mind to thrash the
both of you and send you back to that dismal owl
with your tails between your legs."

"You can't intimidate us," the beaver informed
her evenly. "We're emissaries from our leader. If you
touch us or fail to appear tomorrow at midday, the
owl will send out his strong-arm forces—the moun-
tain lions and the wolf pack—to drag you bodily.
There is no escaping the long paw of justice."

With that, he and the raccoon turned on their
heels like a couple of wooden soldiers and strutted
off, their mission completed. They were so ludi-
crously self-important that Renarda couldn't help
but laugh at their departing backs.

"But, Renarda," whispered nervous Lapine,
"what are we going to do?"

"Don't worry so much, my friend," the fox told
her. She put her paws gently alongside Lapine's soft
neck. "We haven't broken any law. And anyway, what's
he going to do with us? Execute us? The other animals would never allow it. Is he going to try to banish
us to exile outside the forest? Not likely, for we're as
protected by the forest shield as he is. We couldn't
leave even if we wanted to."

Lapine was only half convinced, but there didn't seem to be anything for it but to go about the day's forage as usual. When they came together again at twilight, Lapine followed Renarda's lead and made no reference to the next day's trial. So as not to worry each other, they kept their anxieties banked like a campfire.

Did their fear or worry show as they lay together that night? If so, it was to be observed in a tightening of their embraces, clinging together for dear life. They stroked each other with special care. Who knew what awaited their love on the morrow, or what they might have to sacrifice? They embraced with the fervor of a couple of soldiers set to do battle the next day.

And yet neither slept very well, prefering to be awake and conscious for this last uncompromised night of love.

They emerged from the lair into the morning light together, no longer requiring the subterfuge of staggered exits. They did not register surprise to find a pair of timber wolves at sentry, dispatched by the owl to escort Renarda and Lapine to the spruce grove.

As the curious group made its way through the northern forest, Lapine and Renarda became aware of the many animals crouched by the trail and watching their passage. The faces of these observers were

unabashedly fearful and fretful, yet Lapine could detect that their feelings were clearly weighted by sympathy for the fox and the rabbit. For all the other animals knew that but for the stroke of fortune, they would be marching off to their own trial.

The owl's spruce grove had in attendance mostly busybodies and spies. Unlike the animals along the trail, who were brimming with sympathy, these court watchers looked appalled and aghast at the sight of the two criminals.

As Renarda and Lapine took their seats side by side on a log, with the timber wolves stationed at either end, the raccoon and the beaver suddenly appeared from behind the spruce. "Hear ye, hear ye," they cried in unison, "the owl's court will come to order."

With that the owl swooped down from his tip-top perch and settled himself on a lower limb. There were no preliminaries.

"You two, Renarda the Fox and Lapine the Rabbit, have violated the supreme law of the forest. Fraternization between two species, especially between two females, is strictly forbidden. Why, if everyone acted as you two have, the rest of us would soon find ourselves depopulated and heading for extinction. What do you have to say for yourselves?"

"Sire," said Renarda straightforwardly and with great deference, "we are just two lowly creatures of the forest who've fallen in love with one another. We seek to make no statement by our actions, nor to influence any other animals to follow our lead. We just want to be left in peace."

"Whoo," sputtered the owl, "Whoo do you think you are, to imagine you can break the chain of nature itself? Of course you don't feel responsible, but that's because you both course with the blood of refugees. Don't deny it. Unlike the First Ones, who have been here since time immemorial in this forest, you have no moral compass. You care only for yourselves. Refugees, without a doubt."

Neither Lapine nor Renarda had the slightest clue what their ancestry was, and in truth couldn't have cared less. But they understood the owl's transparent ploy in all of this, to turn them into scapegoats. The owl ruffled his lower feathers into something resembling a sorcerer's robe. "It's time we engineered a separation here, putting these refugee outlaws out of the way of us law-abiding creatures of the forest. I therefore propose two prison camps, one in the northern region of our forest, one in the southern river valley. There my faithful wolves and black bears will patrol the perimeters—keeping the criminals herded."

"O Great Horned One," declared Renarda fervently, "the last thing we want to do is to challenge the laws of nature. Lapine and I would gladly go into internal exile together, so as not to be a burden to anyone else." Lapine was most impressed by Renarda's legal skills and eloquent argument.

"I'm afaid you've got it all wrong," the owl grumped in return. "A typical refugee fantasy, I might add. No, the two of you will be sent to different camps and never see one another again. If either of you is ever deemed to be rehabilitated into understanding of your proper place and your proper affections, you may be invited back to the general population. But I wouldn't count on it."

In that scaring moment, Renarda and Lapine saw how very hopeless their situation was. As the wolf sentries started approaching them from either side, they realized they wouldn't even be allowed to embrace good-bye. Now they were being dragged off out of the spruce grove in different directions, and in the midst of their copious weeping all Renarda had the chance to whisper was "I'll find you."

The owl gloated with power, having proven he

meant business in solving this refugee mess. "Let this be a lesson," he announced to the assembled spies and snitches. "We will make the forest safe for normal creatures."

With that he swooped back to the top of the spruce to savor what he had done. Nothing marred his overweening pride except the steady hot breeze from the southwest quarter, but in the flexing of his power he had pretty well learned to ignore it.

And so the fox and the rabbit went downcast into exile—Renarda into the northern wastes, Lapine into the southern river valley. Both heartbroken. No other animal wanted to greet or know them—not so much because they were what the owl had declared unnatural as because they feared taint by association. The owl's spies were everywhere.

But the lovers did have one stroke of luck. The big brown bear that Renarda had flirted with before Lapine took pity on the lovers, and agreed to serve as messenger between them. The fox filled the bear's ears with endearments, and the blushing bear bounded through the forest to deliver them. The bear was too big to tangle with, so the spies left her alone. And when she reached Lapine, she poured the endearments before her like honey. Lapine was of

course grateful, but in the end no professions of love
and fealty could staunch her sadness. The witch who
had cast the Spell over the forest was gone and could
not help them. For it would take a wizard or sorcerer
to change their fate now, and the forest was fresh out
of sorcery.

BUT NOT THE WORLD OUTSIDE. A full day's
journey from the enchanted forest, in the southwest
region of the barren outside land, where the wind
blew hot, lay an ancient monastery. Once it had nes-

tled in virgin woods of its own, but the greed of lumbermen had reduced its landscape to a desert. And all the monks had fled as well, dispersing to find themselves another green wilderness, leaving behind a lowly student wizard to guard their books till they should send for them.

The wizard's name was Albertus the Lesser, and *he* knew as well as anyone that he hadn't attained anything like status. But he was a studious boy, and he applied himself to read all the vellum folios in the scriptorium, especially the ones on magic. He still couldn't boil water, but he'd managed to map the world into all its zones of sorcery.

It was in the course of his studies one day that he came across a padlocked volume of *Pagan Nature Spells*. It was so tattered and falling apart that he quite easily broke the lock. The text was written in medieval Latin, so he stumbled as he read, a dictionary open beside him. The book listed by country and then by wizard all the various enchanted trees and lakes and meadows. It didn't say which of the spells was still in force, nor did it give the first clue how the spells were set—how much was abracadabra, how much legerdemain.

Since he was looking to discover the recipes for

various acts of magic—the how-to rather than the what—he made as if to close the heavy tome of nature spells. Then his eye was suddenly caught by an ancient map that included the very monastery he lived in. Plotting the coordinates, he realized that within half a day's journey northeast was a whole vast forest brimming with enchantment. The sorcerer was listed as a witch, the Spell a mighty surge of power, 10.0 on the intensity scale, a perfect score. The listing even indicated that the Spell required such a welter of force that the witch herself succumbed in the act of calling it down.

So close, murmured Albertus the Lesser. With scarce a moment's contemplation, he decided he must go there and experience it himself. He'd been too long cooped up in the musty scriptorium. It was, he declared to himself, time for a little field work.

He began by climbing to the top of the monastery's bell tower so he could check out what lay beyond his own fresh desert. Sure enough, to the northeast he could see a green belt across the horizon, something he'd never noticed before. Then he scurried back down the stairs, threw open an ancient trunk of clothes, and wrapped himself up for travel, sporting a midnight blue cape awash with a field of tarnished gold stars. A sorcerer's pointed hat completed the effect. He *looked* the part, even if he couldn't guarantee backing it up with magic of his own.

As he headed through the barren hills where nothing grew, he noticed a hawk circling above him. The hawk had apparently decided on his own to protect the tyro magician, taking pity on his want of power. Albertus appreciated the vote of confidence, waving up at the hawk. He'd always dreamed of having his own familiar.

They crossed an empty, wrinkled riverbed and skirted a former swamp, now parched as well. Beyond the arid former farmland Albertus could see the bone-yard where generations of animals gathered to die.

It was only as he drew closer to the witch's forest that he understood how dramatically she had protected her home ground. He was excited just to behold the effects of such an exercise of power.

Yet the closer he came, till he could almost reach out and touch the first trees, the stranger he found his behavior to be. Striding toward the forest, he suddenly changed his mind, abruptly turned north, and started walking toward a pile of tumbled rocks. He set his pace again toward the forest, and once again veered off, this time to the west, as if some force had skewed his internal compass. After two more unsuccessful passes, he lifted his sorcerer's hat and scratched his head.

This must be part of the Spell, he thought. Then he took a sudden step back as he noticed a grinning tiger in the trees at the edge of the wood. At first fear coursed through him, but then Albertus gave a scornful laugh. *There are no tigers around here,* he scoffed, then realized just how clever was the witch's spell. She'd created a phantasm of fear to keep interlopers from trespassing. That, along with the power to change a man's compass, kept strangers in abeyance, then turned them around. In the days when all this countryside was forested it was easy to cut people off and convince them they *preferred* to go another way, into some other woods.

Albertus settled the sorcerer's hat firmly on his head and moved forward with new resolve. When his inner voice told him to change direction, he stubbornly resisted. *Straight on,* he kept telling himself as he slogged forward through the shield, feeling as if he were trudging through something like pudding. And then he was suddenly through the mire and standing firm on the forest floor. He blinked at his own cleverness.

"You lost your bird," observed Renarda, stepping out from behind a tree.

She was right. He could barely make out the speck of the hawk's wings as it pushed away south, unable to follow. "But you must be a very great wizard, to break through the shield. How did you do it?"

"First of all," Albertus corrected modestly, "I am not a great anything—though I *am* a wizard in training. All I did was apply my mind to the task, and I walked right through. It helped of course to realize you couldn't possibly be a tiger."

Renarda shook her ears in some confusion: this man was doubtless clever, but he talked in circles. "But why exactly are you here? Are you acquainted with the owl?"

"And what owl would that be?" Albertus asked.

"Why, the owl who is our leader, of course. The owl that cast this spell we live in, protected from the world."

Albertus shook his head. "Madam Fox, I fear you are misinformed. It was a *witch* who cast the Spell of the forest shield—a very selfless witch, I might add, for she sacrificed her life to put it in place."

Renarda knit her brows. She was properly stumped. Instinctively she believed this bright young man, whose garb and manner showed he was no woodsman or hunter. She permitted herself a faint gleam of hope.

"Tell me about this owl," Albertus inquired skeptically. "Sounds like a fraud to me."

Oh, gladly did Renarda spin the story of the owl's authoritarian ways. The gathering of all the tribes by the river under that full moon. The splitting up of the denizens of the forest into First Ones and refugees. The use of spies and snitches. And finally, the tale of Renarda and Lapine—their love, their arrest and trial, and their fateful internal exile. Renarda tried to tell her story without emotion, but the tears came anyway. Albertus could hear the quaver of despair in her voice.

He drew his starry cape closer about him and began to pace in a tight circle. He knew there was something wrong with what the owl was doing to this forest. But did he want to get mixed up in it, especially with his power so tenuous? He took in Renarda's heartbroken visage and knew that he could not shirk the challenge. Albertus was as much in training to be a knight as to be a magus.

"Well, first we have to find your friend the rabbit," he announced. "So we can present a united front when we march on the owl."

"How can you be so sure of yourself? He has an army of spies at his command."

"But we have the truth," Albertus countered, leading the way toward the river valley. "No witch *I* ever heard of cared a jot how her animals lived and took their pleasure. After all, witches are themselves chameleons. Some days they're men, some days they're women. They seek to *free* their animals, not rein them in. Your owl is just a big impostor."

Renarda felt encouraged, though she still worried about the owl's reserves of power. Could this boy really summmon up the magic to counter the owl's fraud? Renarda knew more of the ways of the forest than the methods of magic. But she so pined for her rabbit friend that any risk was worth taking that would give her the chance to be with Lapine once more. She would slip from her unnatural exile to accompany the boy wizard to see the owl.

Within a few hours they had reached the river valley, and when Lapine saw her beloved she came leaping over to embrace her. They held each other so tightly that they breathed as one creature. Damn what the guards would say!

Excitedly Renarda introduced Albertus, and in her exhilaration, she swore he had the magic at his

fingertips that would depose the owl forever. Albertus went "Ahem" and tried to play down his sorcery skills, but the lovers were so delirious that he left their hope alone.

Because Renarda and Lapine had a sorcerer between them, the wolves and bears decided to let them proceed on their quest. Indeed, the guardian class of the wilder beasts had not been entirely comfortable in its role as jailers. It impinged on their own freedom as much as on the prisoners'. Deep down inside, they cheered the fox and the rabbit for finding themselves an advocate. Their jailers wished them every success.

"But what are you going to *say*?" asked Lapine, who'd finally found her breathless voice.

"Well," observed Albertus, as they threaded their way through the forest, "first I'm going to accuse him of presenting someone else's work as his own. And then I expect I'm going to have to challenge him in a duel of magic, to prove my credentials, as it were."

This part sounded rather more sketchy altogether, and Renarda shot him an anxious sidelong look. "What sort of magic will you do?" she inquired politely.

"Oh, whatever comes to hand at the time," he

replied with a breezy laugh. "I'm a very spur-of-the-moment sort of magus."

Each of them kept his worries to him- or herself, because it was too late to turn back now. They whistled all the bird calls of the forest and generally tried to buck themselves up. But the closer they came to the owl's spruce grove, the more somber and tentative they became. As soon as they entered the glade, the beaver and the raccoon stared at them, stunned— the fox and the rabbit were breaking the rules of exile! They began to caterwaul at the base of the owl's tree—who was in the middle of a very pleasant nap and didn't want to be bothered.

Grumbling, the owl shook his feathers and swooped down, immediately seeing what was wrong. "*Whoo,*" he bellowed. "*Whoo* has dared to break the exile of these criminals? Who has allowed these vile refugees to mingle once again with First Ones?"

"I believe that would be me," retorted Albertus cheerfully.

"And *whoo* might you be?" the owl countered, "And how did you get through the shield?" There was strain in the owl's voice, as if he had a mouse bone lodged in his gullet.

"I'm just a lowly apprentice wizard, O Great

Horned One. And I have studied the witch's protec-
tive spell from every angle, till I figured out a path
through the shield. You see, it was mostly a matter
of trusting my heart. Which is also why I have
come to defend the love match between Renarda
and Lapine."

"And what witch would you be refering to?"
snapped the owl irritably.

"Why, the witch that cast this magic spell in the
first place." Albertus looked him straight in his yellow-
orange eyes. "Though you have taken all the credit for
the Spell, you know very well you had nothing to do
with it. I'd guess you were the witch's familiar—a
perfectly honorable position, but one that carries not
a drop of power."

The owl's eyes grew wider and wilder, till they
covered half his face in a great scowl. "Guards," he
shrieked, "stop this man and his lies. He is to immediately go into exile along with these so-called lovers."
His voice ended his sentence in a curl of disgust.

But nobody made a move in the wizard's direction. Every creature in the grove seemed fascinated
by this whole altercation, even the usually chattering
beaver and raccoon. Albertus was quick to grasp the
advantage. "Don't you think, O Great Horned One,

that we should settle this matter with a show of sorcery? After all, if you engineered this whole shield by yourself, you must have powers to burn."

"I do not engage in dumb shows with amateurs," the owl shot back.

"Oh, but I think your subjects would consider it a privilege to watch you at work. Wouldn't you?" Albertus glanced around the clearing, which had by now filled up considerably. The animals seemed afraid to nod or speak an opinion, but they were clearly riveted by the whole idea of a duel between owl and this strange and boyish wizard.

Albertus bowed politely to the owl. "After you."

For a moment it seemed as if the owl would defy him, armoring himself in the majesty of his own secure position. Then, suddenly deciding to take the dare, he spread his wide wings and swooped to the top of the spruce again. He crowed with self-confidence as he surveyed his kingdom. "From here," he shouted down to them, "I can see to the farthest limits of the forest. All the animals in the glorious round of their stalking and hunting. The family groups at play, the tribal groups as they extend their territories. The whole teeming pulse of life in the woods, all under my protection."

"Good eyes," murmured Albertus to Renarda and Lapine. "Not quite the same as vision, though."

He watched the owl swoop down to the lower branch again, beside himself with preening. "Now you, wizard," he spat out with contempt, "show us your amateur magic act."

Renarda and Lapine looked very troubled, losing faith by the minute. Blinking beneath his oversized hat, their young and gangly sorcerer seemed barely capable of knotting his own cape neatly, much less even minor magic. But they had not counted on Albertus's keen mind, the result of a boyhood spent among books and potions, studying furiously. He had decided to try to take on some of the Spell's intensity, to lift a portion of the burden from the witch so that she could finally get some peace. He wasn't at all sure he could summon the physical force of the Spell by sheer concentration alone—but he knew his motive was pure, and perhaps the strength of his heart would carry him through. He hunched down into his sorcerer's robe and pulled his pointed cap farther down on his forehead. He sweated and strained, his pale eyes darkening as he focused far into the distance.

Nothing happened. He only had one fear, that in taking on the responsibility for the shield he would weaken it and leave it open to interlopers, damaging it irreversibly. He cleared his mind of everything else and tried to get back to the witch's pure idea. As the minutes went by, the owl and the raccoon and beaver began to boo and hiss. "He has no powers, O Great Horned One," squabbled both the owl's familiars. "Send him into exile."

But the rest of the crowd in the clearing stood silent and stock-still, watching Albertus as he nearly turned himself inside out with concentration, adding his power and youth to the force the witch had left for the forest.

And all of a sudden something *did* begin to happen. From the heap of last year's leaves and twigs, the winter's furze and detritus, came a fluttering and thrashing. As Albertus sat hunched before them, a dance of deliberation in his blazing eyes, first one bony hand and then another emerged from the leaf meal. And as the crowd watched dumbfounded, the witch sat up. She was somewhat the worse for wear, of course, after so many years in the open, prey to the rain and snow, but her eyes flashed as alert as ever, missing nothing.

The first thing she did was stare at Albertus, knowing instinctively he had taken from her some of

the Spell's burden. Falteringly, terrified she was wrong, she spoke to him with her last flutter of hope: "Are you . . . is it possible . . . could you be the Other I've been waiting for?"

"O Gracious Witch, I'm not at all sure I'm worthy to be the Other you speak of. I am still in training, a rank amateur, though my heart is good."

"But you are the first to try to lift the burden, to give me back some life. Till you came along, I couldn't so much as wriggle my toes." She rose almost steadily to her feet. "Now, tell me, what can I do for you?"

Albertus didn't hesitate. "Well, to start with, you can expose this owl as an impostor, for taking sole credit for your magnificent shield, ignoring your passion and altruism."

"This is treason," grumbled the owl, though no one apppeared to be listening.

"You," said the witch, pointing a bony finger at the owl. "You were always a most indifferent and jealous familiar, just waiting for me to drop a stitch. And now you have filled up my woods with spurious rules and called some of my creatures second-class citizens. *You're* the one that belongs in exile. If we allow the generals to decide the laws, then we are no better off than all the forests full of hunters and lumbermen."

With that the owl took off—a knot of bitterness in his chest. Even the beaver and the raccoon did not deign to follow him, wanting to put some distance between the owl and their own gullible fervor.

Still the witch, now sitting on a log and plucking weeds from her tangled hair, could not stop staring at Albertus, as if in him she had summoned something far beyond magic. "But what can I do for *you*?"

"You can bless the union between Renarda the Fox and Lapine the Rabbit, since they were the ones who were punished and sent into exile for love."

"Consider it done. May they be blessed a hundredfold for their daring and their honest hearts. But, Albertus, isn't there something you alone covet?"

"Yes," he said haltingly, "there is. I would be honored to serve as your apprentice, O Great Witch."

"The honor would be all mine. My motives in the Great Spell were not so very pure. I lost the world in the process because there was no one of my kind to love me. Do you think you could love me, Albertus?"

"Oh, but I already do. I have loved you ever since I saw in my book of spells what a vast tract you had set aside to protect the creatures of the forest. I just don't know if I can keep up with you, being such a dabbler."

As the witch went on unweaving the burrs and nettles from her long tresses, she grew more and more to resemble a forest nymph. When Albertus came over and kissed her hands, a wild cheer went up in the forest clearing. Lapine and Renarda hurried to gather wildflowers to garland her hair, and soon the proceedings began to resemble a wedding.

Sitting side by side on the hollow log, hands entwined, Albertus and the witch could neither of them believe their good fortune. The Great Spell of the Forest Shield lay perfectly balanced between them, for now it was the power of love that held it together, a much greater bond than any sorcery the witch possessed on her own.

Sheepishly, Albertus leaned over, even as the animals danced in circles about them, and murmured, "Dearest, I have to admit, I don't even know how to transform myself as a woman. I'm afraid you'll be stuck with me as a man through all eternity."

"Don't be silly," she laughed in delight. "The gender spell is the easiest one of all. It's just a matter of knowing what you want to play."

With that Renarda and Lapine dragged them to their feet to join the dancing. Witch and wizard, fox and hare, and all the other animals—the dancing went on in whirling circles in the spruce grove, while above them floated a hundred birds in full song, till darkness fell and the spruces filled with fireflies, lighting the night.

For three days and three nights running they danced, and not just to celebrate the wedding of the Witch and her young Apprentice. They were cheering the restoration of their freedom, a freedom most of them didn't even know they'd lost. To go whichever way their hearts should lead them, to be nobody but themselves.

Here at least, in the last forest—not the very last perhaps, but the last *unspoiled*—no matter how drear and desert grew the world outside, or how rigid the footfall of every animal out there, here at least the heart would rule, and the Spell go on forever.